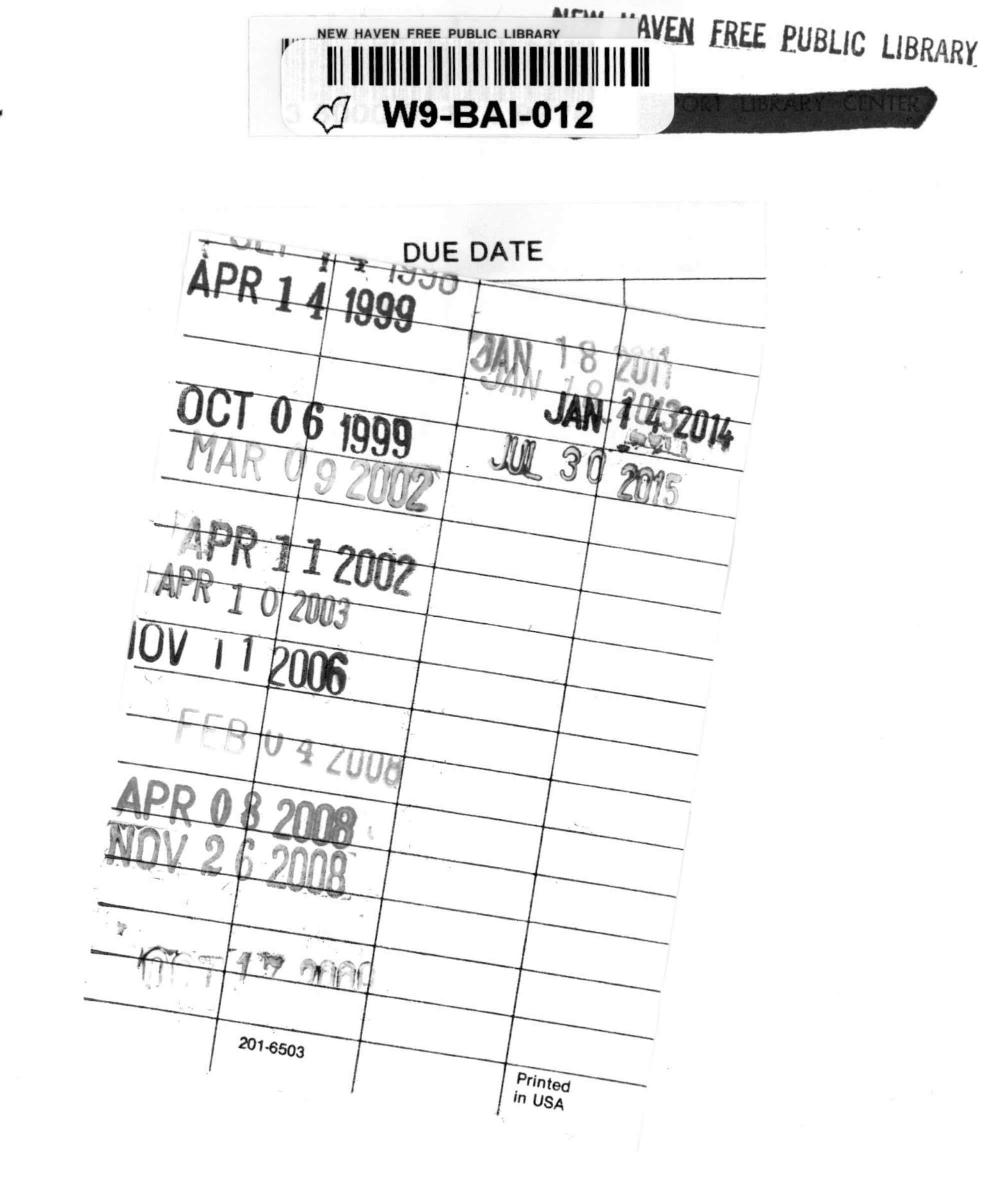
NEW HAVEN FREE PUBLIC LIBRARY
W9-BAI-012
NEW HAVEN FREE PUBLIC LIBRARY
DUE DATE
APR 1 4 1999
JAN 18 2011
OCT 0 6 1999
JAN 1 4 2014
MAR 0 9 2002
JUL 3 0 2015
APR 1 1 2002
APR 1 0 2003
NOV 1 1 2006
FEB 0 4 2008
APR 0 8 2008
NOV 2 6 2008
201-6503
Printed in USA

Little Bear's New Year's Party

By JANICE

Illustrated by MARIANA

Lothrop, Lee & Shepard Company / New York

 Inquiries should be addressed to Lothrop, Lee and Shepard Company, 105 Madison Ave., New York, N.Y. 10016. Printed in the United States of America.

2 3 4 5 77 76 75 74

Janice.
Little Bear's New Year's party.
SUMMARY: Little Bear gives a New Year's party and welcomes more guests than he invited.
[1. Animals—Stories] I. Mariana, illus. II. Title.
PZ10.3.J28Li [E] 72-5234
ISBN 0-688-40002-7
ISBN 0-688-50002-1 (lib. ed.)

It was the day after Christmas and Little Bear, Squeaky the Mouse, Owl, Squirrel, and Sparrow were sitting on Little Bear's floor, eating their Christmas presents.

Little Bear was eating honey. Squeaky was gnawing a piece of cheese. Owl was eating a hamburger specially made for him by Little Bear. Squirrel was eating peanut butter, and Sparrow was eating sunflower seeds.

"I am going to bed as soon as I've finished this pot of honey," said Little Bear, "but I wish it was Christmas everyday."

"But if it was Christmas everyday you would never have New Year's," said Owl.

"What's New Year's?" asked Little Bear. "Do you get presents for New Year's?"

"No," said Owl, "but you have a party. You eat and drink and sing and dance. . . ."

"Until the clock strikes twelve times, and then the new year starts," said Squeaky.

"And everybody says, 'Happy New Year,' and everybody kisses everybody," said Owl.

Little Bear's eyes shone.

"Have you ever been to a New Year's party?" he asked.

Owl shook his head sadly. "No one has ever invited me, but I looked through Mr. Smith's window when he was having one and it looked wonderful."

"Have you, Squeaky?"

Squeaky shook his head sadly. "No one has ever invited me either," he said, "but in the house where I live, they have one every year and I can hear them. It sounds wonderful."

"We've never been invited either," said Squirrel and Sparrow together, "and we haven't even seen one through a window."

"No one has ever invited me either," said Little Bear, "but maybe that was because I was always asleep. I'll go right away and ask someone to invite me to a New Year's party."

"You can't ask anyone to invite you, Little Bear," said Squeaky.

"Why not?" asked Little Bear.

"Because it's not good manners," said Squeaky.

So Little Bear waited patiently for three days for someone to invite him to a New Year's party. But no one did. So, on the fourth day, he decided not to wait anymore. He went out to look for someone who would invite him.

He went to Jake the Pig, Dolly the Mole, Ginger the Cat, and Dicky the Duck. And he asked each one, "Are you inviting any friends to a New Year's party?" Every single one of them said no.

Little Bear was discouraged. It was the last day of the old year. The new year would begin that very night when the clock struck twelve times, and he wasn't invited to a New Year's party!

Little Bear went home. He dragged his feet and hung his head. Squeaky, Owl, Squirrel, and Sparrow could see by the way he looked that no one had invited him. They felt sorry for him. Everybody sat around in silence.

Suddenly Little Bear jumped up and said, "You know what? I'll give a New Year's party myself and I'll invite all of you!"

"Little Bear, do you mean it?" cried Squeaky. He jumped up, clapped his paws and danced around the room, waving his tail in the air. Owl opened and closed his eyes very fast, Squirrel leaped from the window sill to the top of the closet, and Sparrow flew around in circles crying, "Cheep, cheep, cheep."

Suddenly Squeaky stopped dancing. "But Little Bear, no one has invited *you* to a New Year's party."

So they all became silent and sad again.

Everyone was invited to a New Year's party except poor Little Bear.

Then Squeaky had an idea. "You know what, Little Bear?" he said. "I'll give a party too and invite you."

"So will I," said Owl.

"And I," said Squirrel and Sparrow together. "And we'll give it in your house so you won't have far to go."

Little Bear had *four* invitations to a New Year's party now. He just couldn't believe it! "Do you mean it?"

He clapped his paws and jumped up and down, singing, "I'm invited to a New Year's party. I'm invited to a New Year's party."

When he stopped singing he said, "Shall we invite anyone else to our party?"

Squeaky said, "Let's each invite just one guest. There's no room for more."

So Little Bear decided to invite his Uncle Big Bear. Squeaky decided on his Cousin Scrapple. Owl chose his Second-Cousin Hoot, and Squirrel and Sparrow, a friend each.

"Sparrow, you go and invite the guests while we get ready for the party," said Little Bear.

So Sparrow flew away to invite the guests.

Little Bear swept the floor very carefully. Owl made the sandwiches, while Squeaky and Squirrel made the lemonade.

When Sparrow came back, everything was ready. They all put on paper hats, and Little Bear said, "Let's begin. My party is in the living room."

"My party is in the kitchen," said Squeaky.

"Mine's in the attic," said Owl.

"Ours is in the bathroom," said Squirrel and Sparrow.

Everyone went to Little Bear's party. Then Little Bear went first to Squeaky's party, then to Owl's party, then to Squirrel and Sparrow's party.

While they waited for the guests to arrive, they ate and drank and sang. Little Bear jumped up and down, and sang, "Boompla Boompla Booompla BOOM!"

Suddenly there was a loud knock on the door.

"That must be my Uncle Big Bear," said Little Bear. But what was his surprise when he saw not only Uncle Big Bear but three other brown bears standing on the doorstep.

HONEY

"I met them on the way," whispered Uncle Big Bear.

"Your uncle told us you were giving a New Year's party, Little Bear," said the first brown bear.

"We've never been invited to a New Year's party," said the second brown bear.

The third bear didn't say anything. He just smiled his sweetest smile at Little Bear and held out a large pot of honey.

"Come right in," said Little Bear. "You are very welcome." He knew how sad it was not to be invited to a New Year's party. So Uncle Big Bear and the other bears squeezed in.

Everybody was eating and drinking, and Little Bear was jumping up and down singing, "Boompla Boompla Booompla BOOM!" when suddenly there was another knock on the door.

"That must be Cousin Scrapple," said Squeaky. But what was his surprise when he saw not only Cousin Scrapple but three other mice standing on the doorstep.

"I met them on the way," whispered Cousin Scrapple.

"Scrapple told us you were giving a New Year's party," squeaked the first mouse.

"We've never been invited to a New Year's party," squeaked the second mouse.

The third mouse just smiled sweetly and held out a cream cheese.

Little Bear and Squeaky looked at each other. They knew how sad it was not to be invited to a New Year's party, so Little Bear said, "Come right in. You are very welcome."

Cousin Scrapple and the three other mice all scampered in and everybody was singing and dancing. And Little Bear was jumping up and down singing, "Boompla Boompla Booompla BOOM!" when suddenly there was another knock on the door.

"That must be my Second-Cousin Hoot," said Owl.

But what was his surprise when he saw not only Second-Cousin Hoot, but two other brown owls, two squirrels, and three sparrows standing on the doorstep.

"I met them on the way," whispered Second-Cousin Hoot.

"Hoot told us you were giving a New Year's party," said the first brown owl.

"We've never been invited to a New Year's party," said the second brown owl.

The squirrels and the sparrows smiled their sweetest smiles and said, "We're friends of Squirrel and Sparrow."

Owl and Little Bear looked at each other. They knew how sad it was not to be invited to a New Year's party, so Little Bear said, "Come right in. You are very welcome."

So everybody squeezed and squeezed until there was room for everybody. The owls and sparrows flew over the heads of the other guests. The squirrels sat on top of the closet, eating nuts. The mice were on the kitchen table, eating cheese. The bears and Little Bear jumped up and down, and Little Bear sang, "Boompla Boompla Booompla BOOM!"

Then, suddenly, the clock began to strike: one, two, three, four, five, six, seven, eight, nine, ten, eleven,

TWELVE ! ! !

"Happy New Year! Happy New Year!" roared Little Bear.

And everybody shouted, "Happy New Year, Little Bear!" Then everybody hugged and kissed everybody else.

Little Bear ran to the door and opened it wide and he shouted as loud as he could,

"Happy New Year to everyone in the world!"